I0606920

Margaret Junkin Preston

Centennial poem for Washington and Lee University

1775-1885

Margaret Junkin Preston

Centennial poem for Washington and Lee University
1775-1885

ISBN/EAN: 9783337223403

Printed in Europe, USA, Canada, Australia, Japan

Cover: Foto ©Andreas Hilbeck / pixelio.de

More available books at **www.hansebooks.com**

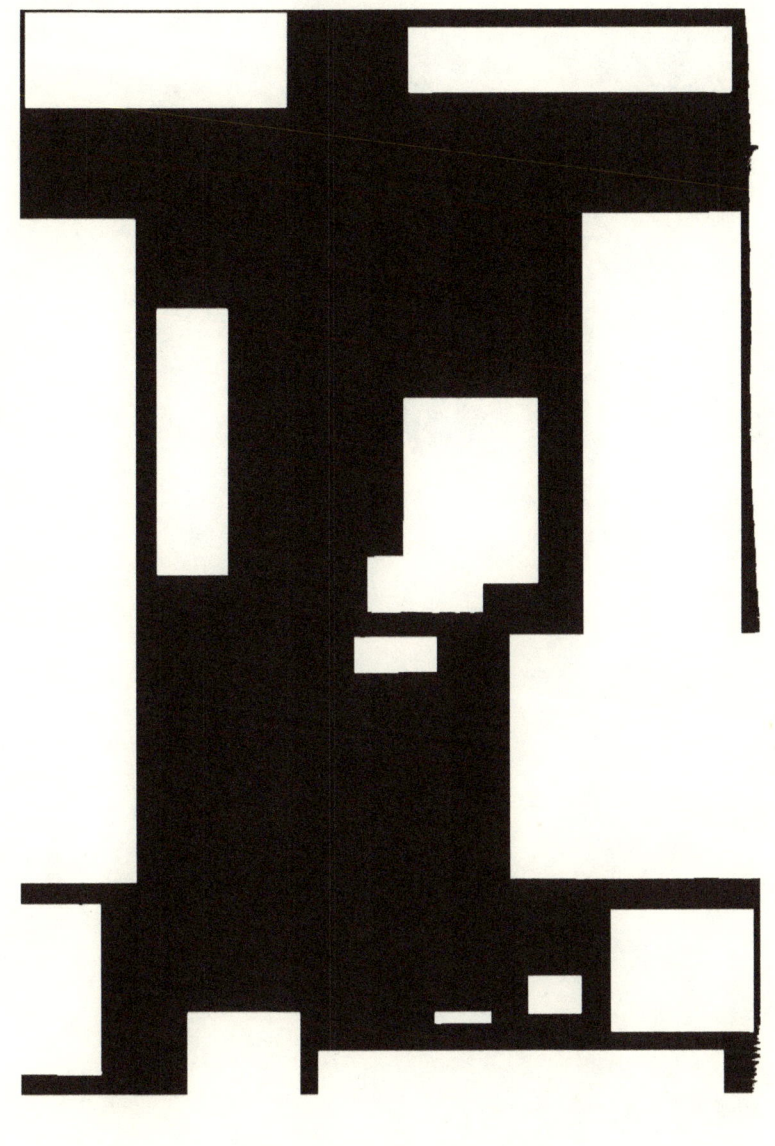

NTENNIAL POEM.

1775–1885.

I.

THE boom of guns was on the air;
   The strong Colonial heart was stirr
     From North to South,
     From East to West,
     From mouth to mouth,
     From breast to breast,
Was passed the inexorable word
That spake a people's last despair
Of England's justice. Everywhere
Brave souls grew braver :—" Let us free
This land for which we crossed the sea,
And make it ours. Revolt may be
The tyrant's name for Liberty ! "
—So flashed the grand electric thought
Through all the Old Thirteen ; so wrought
The current mounting high and higher,
Till eyes were all ablaze with fire

Th███es men heroes—waiting for
Th███read reveille of war.
An███hat April day was done,
Wa███the shot whose startling sound
We███ing all the world around—
███e battle-shot of Lexington!

II.

By yonder stream whose quiet flow
Glides onward toward the silvery James,
More than one hundred years ago,
Were gathered men whose stalwart frames
Defied the winter's frost and snow.
Not as the gallant Spotswood's knights,
With blare of trump and roll of drum,
And floating pennon did they come,
To climb yon Blue-Ridge heights.
What cared such strong-souled men as they,
For knighthood's bauble of a day?—
High-purposed men, to whose keen view
The order of " The Golden Shoe "
Seemed but the Governor's toy! Their eyes
Were stern with thoughts of such emprise

As conquered forests, clothed the hills
With harvests, reared the whirring mills
By every stream ; they nursed a scorn
For the gloved softness of the Court,
Where guarded hands disdained the hard
Grasp of the axe, and found their sport
In tennis-court and tilting-yard ;
They made the valleys laugh with corn,
And purpled with the royal grass,
The meadows, edged with fringing rills,
And opened up the mountain pass :
      Strong men of mould,
      Like vikings old,
Who dared to die, by field and flood,—
Upon their dinted shields, no crests,
No golden Orders on their breasts,
      But—iron in their blood !

III.

So, not to Spotswood's gay and martial band,
Were these beholden for their land
Of Eschol richness. They had felt
Their way along its streams and vales,

3

sky dales ;
its length and breadth h
ltars, offering there
incense of their constant p

IV.

These were the men—McDowells, Lyles,
The Alexanders of "The Isles,"
McLaughlins, Grahams, Campbells, Reids,
Moores, Stuarts—men of doughty deeds ;
Of true blue blood as ever wet
The veins of a Plantagenet !
Here, where to-day we stand, that day they stood,
With axe and shovel, chain and rod,
Prepared to stake the virgin sod ;
And when they paused, and asked what name
Should crown their clearing in the wood :—
They bowed as men would bow in prayer,
For still that echo stung the air,
And warned them of the strife begun :—
What but the now heroic one
That kindled every heart to flame?
What word but—LEXINGTON !

V.

Baptized in blood—named in the name
Triune—a godhead, one, the same—
Religion, Learning, Freedom—here
They chose the spot on which to rear
Humanities more purely true
Than Grecian porches knew ;
      Philosophy and Art,
Nobler than ancient sages could impart ;
Wisdom beyond what Attic scrolls supply,
That taught men how to live, and how to die !

VI.

Upon the timbered ridge that lay
Across the billowy hills away,
There sprang a lowly Academe,
So rude, that no enthusiast's dream
Could have foreshown the fame it rears,
Beneath its century's weight of years ;
      A spring beneath an oak,
      That falling leaves might choke ;
But destined so to broaden far and wide,
That on its bosom argosies might ride !

How arrogant the name bestowed
By Graham in his zeal—" The Hall
Of Liberty " * !—when over all
The land, oppression scored its trace,
Leaving its lines on every face—
> On every heart its load.
> A name prophetic still !
> Since from this classic hill,
Such hero-thoughts and words and deeds have
flowed,
As make it what to-day we see—
To old traditions true, with welcome free,
And doors wide-set—The Hall of Liberty !

VII.

Pure fame ! True name !—When Tarleton flung
His angry and contemptuous taunt
Against the Valley, did it daunt
The cleric Captain † in that hour
Of onset ?   Did his spirit cower
Beneath it ?   Nay !   When proud and clear,

---

* Afterwards Washington College.
† The Rev. Wm. Graham, first Rector of Liberty Hall and Captain of the Liberty Hall Company.

His Chieftain's summons reached his ear—
" *Up ! Men of West Augusta !* " quickly down
Each ardent scholar flung his books and gown,
Snatched up his musket, girt his sword,
And rushed to drive the British horde
Beyond the Piedmont.

VIII.

When the day
Of triumph came, and war's surcease
Made room for holy arts of peace,
Our Cincinnatus nobly laid
The proffered wealth he would not claim,*
Down at " The Hall," whose well-won name
Had reached him 'neath Mount Vernon's shade,
And stirred his heart : Not yet, not yet,
Could he forget
His " Men of West Augusta ! "

IX.

Turn and see
" The Ruins " yonder, lichened with decay,†

---

* Washington endowed " Liberty Hall " with a large grant voted
to him by the Legislature of Virginia.
† The old stone College destroyed by fire in 1803.

Where dreaming students stray,
Recalling visions of the elder day.
The log-hewn " Hall " has grown to be
Collegian in its state ; the one
Foremost and first of all to bear
The name that since has filled the air ;
That stirs the world's heart to its core,
As never name had done before ;
The name that swells the Poet's song ;
That makes humanity sublime ;
That teaches patriots to be strong ;
That heads the warrior-list of time ;
Repeated since ten thousand ways,
Which yet no speech of every day's
Most common use can rob of praise ;—
That name which, like the sun,
Loses no light by all it rests upon ;
Which glorifies with gorgeous alpen-glow
Mont Blanc's stark summits of eternal snow ;
Yet gilds the crocus blossoming below :
        —The Name of WASHINGTON !

X.

I

Not from the ilex groves where Sophocles
  Chanted his strophes grand,
Not from the slopes where silvery olive trees
  Flung shadows o'er the land ;

2

Not from the garden seats where Plato taught,
  Not from the Bema's height,
Did the young Greek look on a landscape fraught
  With such a rare delight.

3

Behind yon isolated mountain crest,
  Draped in the filmy fold
Of trailing clouds whose splendor hung the west
  With broidery-work of gold,

4

The musing scholar watched the sun go down,
  Bequeathing near and far,
With sovran hand, to every peak a crown
  Translucent as a star.

5.

He looked from off the classic page, all flushed
    With mists of Attic rills;
And saw Virginia's loveliest valley hushed
    In her embracing hills.

6.

What serried corn !   What fields of amber grain !
    What haunted homes were there !
—Not Arcady, with Pan and all his train
    Was ever half so fair !

XI.

Shades of the Past ! we see you file
With pensive step and serious face,
Each to his own appointed place
Within the Academic aisle.
Wise Alexander's look of peace
Turned heavenward ; Crittenden whose name
Lights up Kentucky's roll of fame ;
Majestic Baxter ; witty Speece ;
Calm Ruffner with his wondrous lore ;
McDowell robed in courtly grace ;

Floyd with his marble-featured face ;
The Southern Preston who could sway
Senates that thrilled before a Clay ;
Grave Plumer with his golden store
Of Saint Chrysostom eloquence ;
Judicious Brown in word and deed,
The Hooker of the Church's need ;
And many a sage and statesman more,
    Went from these haunted precincts hence,
    Whose names the bead-roll bore.*

XII.

Peace needs no history : Year by year,
The placid seasons came and went ;
And in their Happy Valley here,
Its dwellers drank, with thankful cheer,
    The wine of sweet content.
They saw with pride the pillared range
Surmount the hill-crest yonder—saw
The reign of order, peace, and law
Prevail within its honored walls,
Without a crave or care for change.

---

* Distinguished graduates.

The yearly stream of graduates passed,
And took their place, well-trained and true,
To do the work that men should do,
Earnest and faithful to the last,—
　In legislative halls ;
In pulpits where the people hung
Entranced on many a silvery tongue ;
In courts where truth and right prevail,
And Justice holds the level scale ;
In chambers where a gracious art
　Avails to stay the laboring breath,
And snatch the throb that stirs the heart
　Out of the grasp of death.
Love trained them in its sweetest lore ;
And Idyls for themselves they made
　In many a lilac shade,
Chanting them to rapt listeners o'er and o'er ;
Idyls yet fonder than Theocrites
　Piped to Sicilia's breeze.

XIII.

Pale students did not ask,
In that unworn and younger day,

To have the edge of their appointed task
By such attrition worn away,
As ball and hop and " German " furnish, when
The temples ache with intellectual pain ;
Or as the evening drive, with two-in-hand,
Beside the fairest lady of the land,
Can bring the over-wrought and throbbing brain !
   Enough for them the quiet walk ;
   The interchange of book and flower ;
   The passing of a moon-lit hour
   Meshed by a maiden's tender talk ;
   The music of the practised tunes
   That hallowed Sunday afternoons ;
   The pathos of the going away ;
   The blush that sealed engagements made
   Beneath the locust's shade,
   For next Commencement Day !
   *   *   *   *   *   *
O days of innocence, forever o'er,
Who sighs to think ye can return no more !

XIV.

But clouds at length began to dim
The country's broad horizon rim ;

Dissensions rose on every hand,
And strained to breaking, the strong strand
Of Brotherhood : And through and through,
By doubts our fathers never knew,
The Nation's inmost soul was wrung.
Fierce taunts from North to South were flung ;
Fanatic meddlers dared to thrust
The pikes they forged in fires of hate,
With crazy strivings to adjust
The fine machinery of state.
And when their rankling injuries stung
The South to madness, what availed
To guard the sacred rights assailed ?
And when the fatal fiat sprung
War on Virginia's borders—when
No choice remained for dauntless men,
What else was left to do or say,
But draw the sword, and Yea or Nay,
Fling, in hot wrath, the sheath away !

XV.

That April morn of 'Sixty-one
Broke sad and ominous ; for the roar

14

That belched from Sumpter's baleful gun,
Echoed from mountain-top to shore,—
  The desperate deed was done !
Then came the startling, stern command :—
" Close up your College doors ! Disband
Your classes once again, and go,
Like Graham's youths, to meet a foe
Stronger than Tarleton's. Seize your guns,
And prove yourselves the patriot sons
  Of patriot sires ! "

XVI.

  Who can forget
With what a fierce and fiery bound
Of heart, they came, when Nelson wound *
War's first alarum ? How they met
With ready step and fervent will
His summons to the daily drill,—
These beardless heroes ! even yet
We seem to hear their measured tread
As on they marched, with lifted head,
Leaving all eyes behind them wet.

---

* Prof. Nelson, first Captain of the College Company.

Brothers in arms, they felt the thrill,
When the hot rider came, who bore
The order to yon martial hill—
" *Send forward Jackson and the Corps !* "
And when to their first field of fight,
Upon Manassas' summer plain
They marched beneath the bullets' rain,
Following the dauntless step of White,*—
What worthier names were 'midst the slain?
What veterans poured a richer flood,
And deeper wrote their names in blood?

XVII.

Draw close the veil! Be dumb!
Let the young martyrs go
Down the memorial years,
With solemn step and slow ;
Nor count the fields of death,
Where, with a courage strong,
As only to the noblest souls belong,
They yielded up their breath.

---

* Prof. White, Captain of the College Company at the first Battle
of Manassas.

Smiles all too proud for woe
Have flashed across our tears,
A grand aërial bow
That spans and circles o'er
Their names for evermore!

XVIII.

Why, then, nurse to life the pain
Of those bitter years again?
Why awake the mournful knell
Of despair that rang abroad,
When the brave young Captain fell,*
Mid the crash of shot and shell,
Slain upon his native sod?
    Or the gallant Pendleton,†
Sank when later fields were won?

XIX.

I

Ah! when with arms reversed,
And shrouded flags, the men

---

* Captain Hugh W. White, who fell at the head of the College
Company, at the second Battle of Manassas.
† Lieut. Col. A. S. Pendleton, of Stonewall Jackson's Staff.

Who followed him the first,
Bore the dead Hero to his home again—

2

The Hero who could thrill
With voice and flash of eye
   Broken battalions till,
With shout and cheer, they rushed straight on to
   die—

3

How could we bear it?—how
Crush down with strange control,
   Despairs whose memory now,
Can even send a shudder through the soul?

4

Ah! Glory, Honor, Fame!
Ye had no power to stay
   The gulfing griefs that came
To wreck our hopes, that ghastly morn in May! *

XX.

Hush the drum!
Stop the blare!

---

* May 15, 1863, the day of General Jackson's burial.

Let the beat
Of sad feet
Cease their tramp along the street:
Let the tolling bell be dumb,
Drive these sounds of fear
Even from Memory's ear;
Lest our lost and wept for come
With a vision of storm and wrack,
Bringing all our heart-break back!

    *   *   *   *   *   *

Thank God! that time has brought us healing balm!
Thank God! for blessed anodynes of calm!

XXI.

The fratricidal strife at last
Wore to its close: our dream was past;
Spiked was the last Confederate gun;
    And Might the day had won.
Our great Commander's pitying soul,
Yielding to Fate's supreme control,
Forebore, within the chasm of strife
To cast another Curtius life,
And bravely owned the dread eclipse

That darkened sky and sun.
Then war-worn veterans weeping heard
As sad, magnanimous a word
As ever left a warrior's lips :—
* * * *" Men ! I have done my best for you*
And you for me ! Our fallen Cause
Demands that you be strong and true,—
Demands that you maintain the laws :
I 've done my very best for you !" * * *
—His *" best" !*—How grand it was !

XXII.

With hopes destroyed, with ties all riven,
With wife and children, exiles driven,
With not another home than Heaven,—
What did our Chieftain ? From his hand
Drop his untarnished sword, and stand
In dark despair and sullen pride,
Within the land he would have died
So gladly for ? Nay ! never he !
To do, and dare, and die, when need
Demanded, this were brave indeed :
For State and Country still

To live, and bow submissive to God's will,—
Only such lofty chivalry
Became the name of Lee !
He knew misfortune's harsh control
Howe'er it bowed, could never break
The mettled spirit that could stake
Its all on Duty,—never take'
True manhood from a human soul !
He listened not to lures of ease
That offered homes across the seas :
What charm had visions such as these
For him, whose oath was sworn to share
All ills his State was doomed to bear ?

XXIII.

—" Come lead us in the paths of peace,
As once in war, since war must cease ;
    And teach us how
    We too may bow ;
And from sown dragon-teeth may raise
A phalanx armed for bloodless fight,
To crush the wrong—maintain the right—
The Sparti of our future days ! "

XXIV.

With grand humility he came,
And found his calm Mount Vernon here,
While the world's pæans crowned his name
With praise he did not turn to hear.
And never in the proudest hour
Of war's embattled pomp and power,
Did he so rule all hearts, and sway
Their reverence as none other can—
The noblest, courtliest gentleman—
    The knightliest knight who wore the Gray !

XXV.

Ye saw him take with matchless grace
The academic seat, and wear
Its humble honors, with such rare
Majestic skill, as if the place
Were broad enough to meet the large demands
    Of his imperial hands !
Ye watched him as his silvered head
Bowed meekly at the morning prayer ;
And marvelled, as with martial tread,
That brooked no swerve to left or right,

His bands of students firm he led
    As legions to the fight !
Ye saw him in his peaceful rest ;
Ye saw him in the evening's wane,
When unobscured by mist or stain,
His cloudless orb went down the west.
    *   *   *   *   *   *
* * * Ah !—scarce we dare beneath our breath,
To name him here—so pure, so brave !
Tread softly ! for the Sculptor's skill
Holds him in seeming slumber still :
Hush !—for that stirless sleep is death,—
Peace !—for we stand too near his grave !

XXVI.

Oh ! ye who tread these classic halls,
Baptized once more in patriot blood,—
Think what exalted memories flood
These doubly consecrated walls !
The hoary lore of Oxford's towers,
Made sacred by her Alfred's name,
Can never boast a prouder fame
Than shrines these simple aisles of ours !

---

* Valentine's recumbent figure in the Mausoleum.

XXVII.

Ye will not walk ignoble ways:
Ye dare not seek unworthy aims :
Ye cannot do a deed that shames
These heroes of our holiest days !
Your oath a Roman oath must be,
Sworn with a faith that will not yield—
Sworn on the doubly sacred shield
   Of WASHINGTON and LEE !